Chosen for You

The Mating Grounds

Ciree Hawthorn

Cover illustration by Mara Val (@scales.n.art)
Interior maps by Robert Gant (robgantart.com)
Editing by EJL Editing (www.ejlediting.com)

CONTENT NOTES

Please be advised that this book contains elements that may be triggering for some readers.

Tropes: Forced proximity, mistaken identity, virgin FMC, he teaches her a skill

Content Warnings: explicit sex, minor jealousy, self confidence doubts, anxiety

To all my anxiety plagued girlies and the cinnamon rolls that calm them :)

Contents

Map

PALMYRA
ENIOS ZONE
AFRAAD ZONE
SKARA
TAXILA
DERDE ZONE
HEMIE ZONE
SANCHI
KEDIA ZONE
CARAL
PRIMUS ZONE
PERIDIA

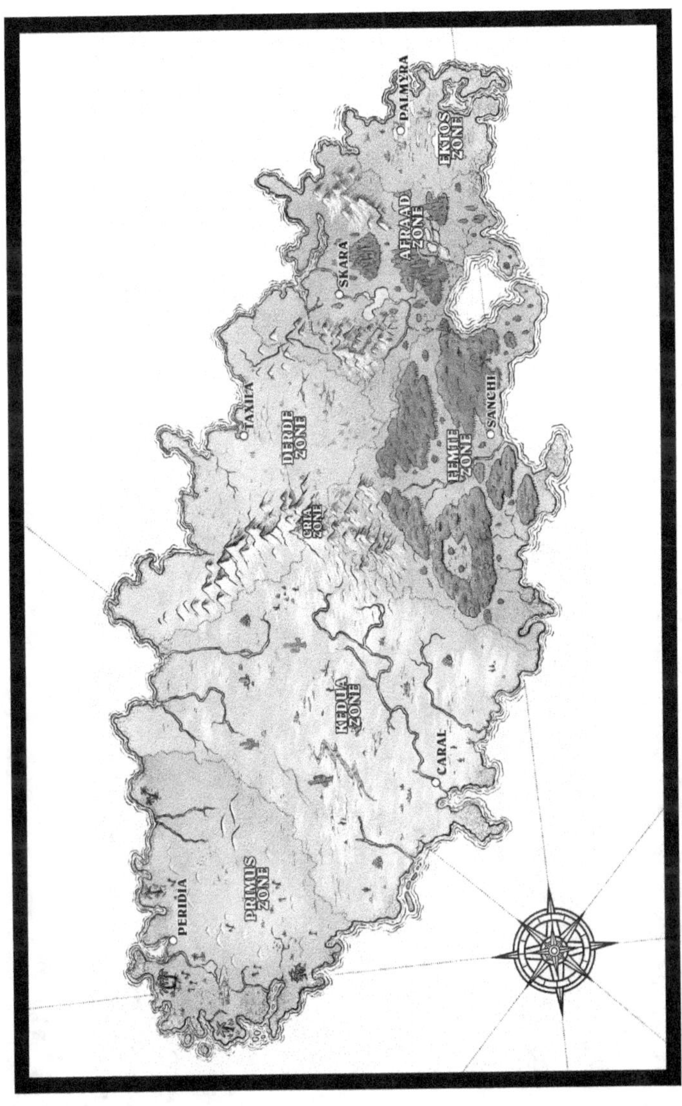

Cria Zone Compound

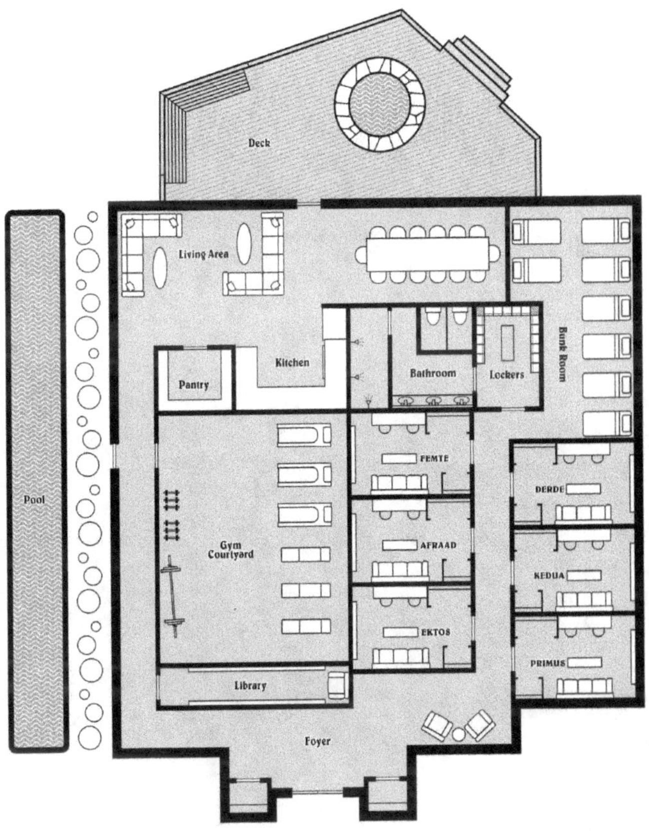

PROLOGUE

The scientists never expected to lose ninety percent of the population to a massive illness, but that's exactly what happened 210 years ago. The continent had been teeming with life, communities and free will and then within a single year, people were crowding into each of the zone's capital cities to share resources and avoid living and dying alone in the scattered ghost towns left behind. People were scared shitless and worried about humanity's survival, so to assuage those fears, the zones came up with a new system.   The Cria Zone, where the Mating Grounds take place, is centrally located on the continent in the high mountains, in order to be accessible to and supplied by all zones. The Chosen journey there after being selected and live in a secure compound for the duration of the year until the mating ceremony, when established pairings are announced and any unattached Chosen are assigned mates. After the mating ceremony, the pairings journey back to the inhabited zones according to the female's origin.

That system is known as the Mating Grounds.

The Mating Grounds are how humanity has survived with so few people left, and avoided inbreeding or extinction—the inevitable outcomes if birth rates dip too low. Every five years, a male and female in their peak reproductive years (aged 18-25) are selected from each zone and sent to the Cria Zone for semi-arranged pairings to help spread their genetic material between the distant cities. The only rules in the Cria Zone?

1. You have one year to find a partner of your choosing before one is assigned to you.

2. Offspring are expected from each pairing.

3. You must choose a partner from another zone.

4. The ruling zone sends four eligible citizens, instead of two, during their

period in power.

Beyond the Cria Zone mandates, each zone handles eligibility and 'love pairings' as they see fit. Between the most and least populous zones the policies can vary greatly based on eligible citizen population numbers.

CHAPTER 1

DAY AFTER THE CHOOSING

Cora

As the female Chosen for the Derde Zone, I'm thrilled to be leaving behind my room in the eligible citizen dorms and my boring job as a government farmhand.

All things considered, I was pretty lucky to have both seeing as my family has lived in the no man's land part of our zone for generations and are pretty isolated. They have chosen to homestead instead of live in community with the rest of the populace. I was sent to Taxila once I was of age—just as my cousins were—to work, learn a bit about city life and be available for the Choosings.

Going from a homestead in no man's land to living here in the city has been no small adjustment. At least at work I know where I stand in the hierarchy and what to do, but the second I get home it's just so loud and you can't get a peaceful moment anywhere with all these eligibles living in one place. Not to mention trying to sleep at night with all the sex being had. It's ridiculous.

Luckily, I am being sent to the Cria Zone for this year's Mating Grounds and get to have my whole life sorted for me. By the end of this year, I'll have a (hopefully) loving partner and a little one of my own on the way.

I'm so happy I got selected because dating is fucking terrifying. I grew up around nobody but my family, how the hell am I supposed to know how to approach someone romantically?!

It's been awful, and the hormones running rampant in the dorms don't make it any easier with everyone just going wild with no supervision. The first week I was here I had three guys approach me with the cheesiest of pick-up lines. As if that was going to seduce me!

Gross. Pass.

After that word must have gotten around that I wasn't into the hookup vibes and people stopped popping in to feel me out for bed sport potential.

The Mating Grounds will be so much easier, everyone knows what they are there for, you know you will leave with someone, so at least there is motivation to find a partner you are actually compatible with right from the start. No weird games of will we or won't we.

My male counterpart that was Chosen with me is one of the pick- up line boys, so help the poor girl he sets his eyes on.

Ronan

As I pull myself out of the water, I see my father gesturing to me in the distance. I grab my towel and quickly swipe at my arms, legs and torso while jogging to meet him on the road back into town.

"You know, of all the days to take a long swim, today was maybe not your best choice son," he lectures as he hands me a shirt and holds onto my shoes and pants while I pull it over my head.

"I needed peace and quiet," I huff back, struggling to dress and walk at the same time.

"And your mother would've loved the time with you. Instead, she was packing her only son's belongings as he gets ready to move away for good." A long sigh leaves my chest, unbidden. Of course, mom's a mess. I should have been more thoughtful about how I spent my last day at home after being Chosen for Ektos.

"I'll write! It's not as if I'm on my deathbed dad."

"Yes, but she likely won't ever get to hug you again, or stay up late talking with you about the boat or what you caught each day. This is a big loss for her, you know. She's been a mother for the last 19 years." I feel his hand reach out to rub my shoulder, and realize he must be feeling the loss too. I grab his waist in half of a hug, pulling him close as we walk.

"I'll always be your son, I'll just be someone's partner and eventually a father myself too."

The seriousness of that doesn't elude me quite as much as it did yesterday when my name was called. As I stood side by side with the only other eligible male in my zone, I knew there was a good chance of being Chosen, but hadn't fully prepared myself for that reality. Now that it's happened, I needed the swim this morning to really meditate on it and make my peace with leaving here and moving on.

As we approach our house, a little thing on the edge of town, lifted high on stilts to avoid the seasonal flooding, I see my mother through the window. She's bent over, adding something to my bags in the entryway. My chest tightens and I bound up the stairs, sweeping her into a massive hug and spinning her around.

"You're getting me all wet! Who raised you?!" She cries as I spin her around again.

"A wonderful mother and father that loved me and didn't care if I tracked in water after my swims," I taunt, trying to keep her smiling. As I set her back down, she examines the small living area, as if making sure I haven't forgotten anything, and I see her expression darken slightly.

"No more tears, Mother. I'm off to find true love, remember?" I grin and shoulder my packs, nodding to my fellow Chosen in the distance that's beckoning me to join her at the main road out of town and to the Cria Zone. Suddenly I recall my childhood crush on her, she's a sweet girl, but utterly wrong for me. I'm glad I shelved that years ago now.

Father snags me into one last embrace and I pull away slowly, trying to keep my expression light and happy for them. "I love you both, and I'll write as frequently as I'm able!" I murmur as I turn to leave and jog back down the stairs.

Don't look back, Ronan. They will think you're already homesick.

CHAPTER 2

DAY OF ARRIVAL IN THE CRIA ZONE

Cora

Today is the day we finally arrive at the Cria Zone. Today I will move into the place where I will meet my future partner. Today the rest of my life finally begins.

No wonder I feel nauseous.

Since this morning it's felt like the inside of my mouth has been sweating. That added to the massive knot in my stomach and my shaky hands are all pointing to a serious upchuck reflex being kicked into high gear.

As I swallow my spit for the millionth time, the Cria Zone compound comes into view and I start walking faster. *Just get through the door, the hardest part is meeting everyone and they shouldn't be here for a day or so.*

Dust flies up around my feet as I power walk the last few minutes, determined to just get in there and figure out the rest as I go. I handled the move to Taxila just fine in the end, this place will have way fewer people to meet and I don't even have to work while I'm here. It'll almost be a vacation. *Not that I've ever had a vacation.*

As I swing the door open and call out a greeting, I hear shuffling down the hallway but nobody replies to my yelled 'hello'. I shift my pack to my other shoulder as I go to investigate the noise.

The hallway is dark and as I hurry along, trying not to run into anything and the shuffling noises are getting louder. I round a bend and see a handful of doorways, each with a zone name above the door itself. The Derde room is at the end of the hall on the right, so I make my way towards it, hoping to set down my stuff.

Just as I pass by the other rooms a door is hurled open and clips my left side.

"Ow!" I shriek in surprise, grabbing my shoulder with my opposite hand and massaging the bruise that is surely forming beneath the skin.

A tall man with wavy brown hair steps through the doorway with a mop in hand, his forehead scrunched together in a surprised wince.

"I'm so sorry! I didn't realize anyone would be here! Are you alright?"

"I'll be fine, you just caught me off guard with the door. I didn't mean to sneak up on you." *Poor guy must be the cleaning crew for the compound. I probably scared him out of his wits if he thinks I've arrived early.*

"No, no, I should've been more mindful. Please, let me help you with your bags." He sets the mop aside and reaches for my bag, twitching his fingers for me to hand it over.

"Oh I don't want to distract you from your task, I can handle this on my own. Thank you for your help around here!" I toss back as I head to the Derde room and shut the door behind me.

Ronan

I have never been happier in my life to have arrived in the Cria Zone early.

Note to self, thank the governor for letting us stow away on the supply caravan wagon in order to get here before everyone else.

Usually, our zone's Chosen arrive in Cria last because of how far we have to travel. Luckily—for me—Ektos has been consistently struggling with birth rates and the governor wanted to give us whatever advantage we could get this round. Getting here first gives us first dibs on any Chosen as they arrive. If we can make a good first impression at least.

My disastrous little run in with the female Chosen was not that.

Now I just need to figure out a way to re-do my shoddy introduction to her, because now that I've met her, I don't really want to meet anyone else.

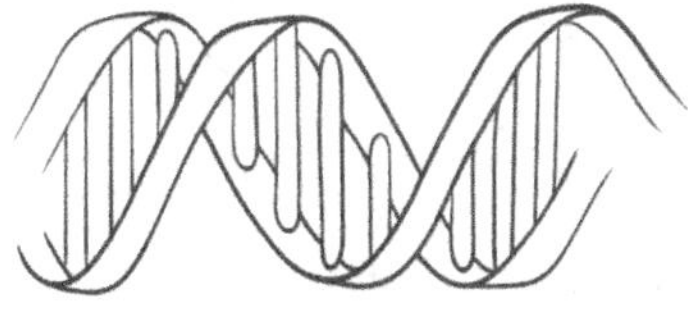

I end up explaining the whole thing to my fellow Chosen from Ektos to get a female perspective.

"So then I accidentally hit her with the door as I was mopping up the water I tracked in after my swim."

"Great start, super attractive," she deadpans.

"Well at least I was cleaning up after myself!" I wail as I cover my face with my hands and flop onto the couch.

"Yes. Kudos. You're an evolved man that cleans. That is actually pretty helpful. It's hitting her with the door that didn't do you any favors, Ronan."

"I know, I know. Now how do I introduce myself properly to erase the memory of that?!"

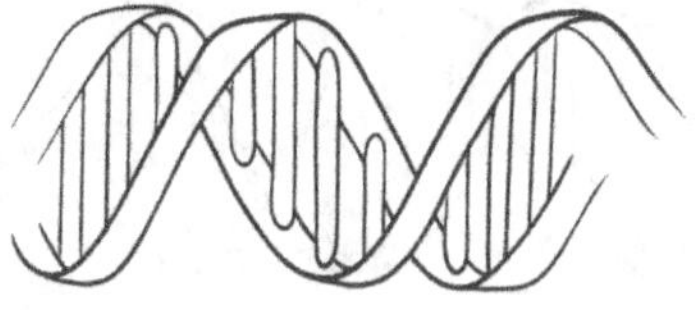

As I approach the Derde room, emboldened by the pep talk, I go through the plan in my head.

Just as I'm about to knock, the door opens a crack and I hear the new female Chosen tell her zone mate she's going to grab lunch in the kitchen. *Change of plans.*

The door opens fully and she steps out.

"Hi. I realized I didn't catch your name earlier. I'm Ronan."

I reach out to shake her hand and she stares at it as I extend it towards her, then flicks her eyes back to my face.

"Wow, I didn't realize you'd be around here often enough to warrant an introduction!" she exclaims, reaching out and shaking my hand.

"Did I read this completely wrong? Would you prefer I wasn't around often?" I slowly step away from her as I realize I might be invading her personal space.

"Well, I mean, as often as you need to be for your job, I suppose?" She shrugs and appears confused.

"I think there must have been a misunderstanding. I'm a Chosen, not staff…"

Her cheeks flush the prettiest red color and her eyes go wide. "I'm an idiot."

"No! No. Not at all. I was cleaning. I was early. I'm sure it all threw you off!" I try to reassure her, stepping back in and putting my hand on her shoulder.

She averts her eyes, shuffling her feet and my stomach flips.

"Would you like to grab lunch together? I was on my way and if you're hungry I can point out all the good stuff I scoped out this morning." I start turning towards the kitchen and pause, allowing her room to refuse if I've just mucked this up even more than before.

"That sounds wonderful actually. Thank you. I'm Cora, by the way."

She follows me down the hallway and I try not to bounce on my feet as I walk. *Her name is Cora.*

CHAPTER 3

4 DAYS AFTER ARRIVAL IN THE CRIA ZONE

Ronan

Cora is adorable. She's shy and nervous, but it all comes off in such an endearing way that I can't help but smile at all her little blushes and stutters. She's started to come out of her shell the past day or two and we have made a habit of grabbing meals together every day.

"Cora, do you want to join me later for a swim? I've been a little nostalgic for home today and thought getting wet might help."

"I'm going to just ignore the blatant innuendo in that statement," she blushes and replies, reaching for her water and gulping it down.

"Oh, holy... Not my intention!" I sputter. "I just meant that I usually swim every day at home and missed yesterday and thought you might want to join me and it came out all wrong and weird. I'm sorry!"

She raises her eyebrows at me. "Well, tempting as you have made it sound, I never learned how to swim. I don't think I'd be very good company."

She goes back to eating and I get an idea.

"Do you want to learn?"

"Oh, I don't know. I don't want to disrupt your swim time with you having to teach me. Besides, what if I'm horrible? I'll look ridiculous compared to you!" Her cheeks go red again at the acknowledgement and I melt a little.

"I love teaching people and it's a survival skill! I'd feel better knowing you knew how. Really, you'd be doing me a favor," I insist, grinning at her like a small child.

Cora

Ronan meets me outside next to the pool and I shiver a bit as an evening breeze blows the edges of my big t-shirt over my thighs.

"I wasn't sure what to wear for this. Promise it won't be weird if I just wear my bra and underwear?" I waver a bit, still unsure if this will come across too strongly. *Not that I have anything else to wear swimming.*

Ronan visibly swallows and shakes his head. "Not at all, it's all the same coverage anyways." He turns and dives into the pool, cleverly avoiding any sort of awkward response from me. I peel the shirt off and sit down at the edge of the pool, easing my feet in first as I adjust to the temperature of the water.

Ronan surfaces after what seems to be forever. *Doesn't he need to breathe?!* He shakes the water out of his eyes and as he does a lock of his wavy brown hair slaps across his forehead and sticks there. I fight the urge to swipe it away.

"Ok, first things first, we will start with floating," he says as he pulls me off the edge and down into the pool.

"I thought I was learning to swim? What use is learning to float?" I demand, reaching for the side to hold on for dear life.

"Well, for one, you can float until help arrives if you find yourself in water unexpectedly. But mainly, it's good to calm you down and get comfortable just being in the water. Once you feel good with that, we can start learning the strokes."

"Ok, that's fair I suppose."

"Are you ready to let go and try then? I promise I'll be right here the entire time," he assures me as he reaches for me and pulls me away from the wall.

His chest is so warm compared to the water around us, and I find myself nestling closer as he describes what he's about to do. The slow beat of his heart thrums against my bare skin as I cling to him and try to listen closely.

"I'll tip you back and support you from underneath while you focus on laying flat and spreading your arms. Just try to keep as flat as you can and remember to breathe."

"Okay, just go slowly."

"Of course," he reassures me as he starts to steer me into more of a horizontal position.

I startle a bit as my equilibrium is disrupted and flail for him, grabbing his neck with one hand and curling in on myself. He keeps one hand beneath my butt and one around the back of my neck, gently directing me to straighten back out.

"See I told you I would be bad at this," I huff.

"You're doing beautifully. Seriously. That reaction was totally normal."

"If you say so," I hedge, working to calm my breathing and lay back.

"I do. And I'm the expert in this situation."

I see his smirk out of the corner of my eye and try not to laugh at his bravado. He's *quite the charmer when he's in his element.*

We practice this way for a few minutes, and I start to feel at peace just floating with his strong arms supporting me. As I'm considering this, I realize that he has pulled back and is no longer holding me up. I'm floating on my own.

I thrash even harder than before and crumple, my peace completely obliterated as I start to sink. Ronan rushes back to my side, scooping me up and holding me close.

"You were floating! You did it Cora!"

My indignation fades as quickly as it rose in my chest, and I grin, proud of myself.

"I was, wasn't I?"

"You were. A speed record for learning to float if I've ever seen one," he jests, squeezing me slightly in an imitation of a hug.

I squeeze my arms around his neck right back. My smile widening with the laugh bubbling out of my chest. I lean in closer to finally wipe that piece of hair from his forehead and he bends down simultaneously, our foreheads meeting.

I feel our breaths quickening, our chests rising faster and faster and I make eye contact. His deep brown eyes are gazing back at me. Just as I'm about to pull away I see him glance down at my mouth.

My breath catches as he tilts my head back slightly and kisses me slowly. His lips feel warm and soft, his hands cradling me against him as I return the kiss.

CHAPTER 4

2 WEEKS AFTER ARRIVAL IN THE CRIA ZONE

Ronan

I catch myself smiling as I round the corner into the living room to meet Cora for breakfast. I've been thinking about what I should make her this morning and I'm leaning towards pancakes. She'll love them.

"Hey, Ronan, what's up?" one of the newly arrived female Chosen—*I think her name is Natalie?*— pipes up from the couch.

"Not much. Just thinking about what to make for breakfast."

"Oh, I'll help, breakfast is my favorite meal!" She squeals as she jumps up from the couch and runs over, pulling a mixing bowl and skillet out of the cupboards and staring at me expectantly.

"Great... Pancakes ok?" I propose, already dreading the moment that Cora walks in and sees me hanging out with this chick playacting domestic bliss.

"Pancakes are perfect! I wonder if they have maple syrup here? We can never get it back home," she ponders, drifting towards the pantry and rummaging around.

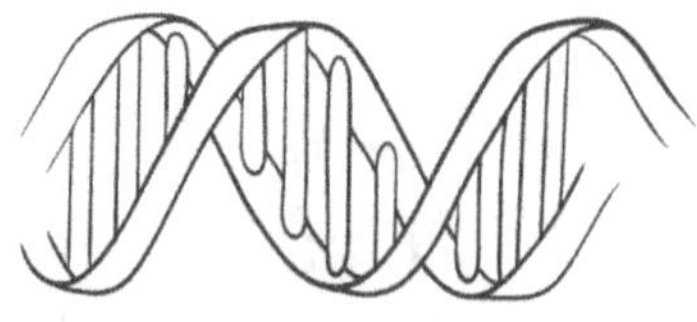

As I finish setting the table and turn to grab the heaping plate of pancakes for the table, Cora finally arrives. She takes one glance at the female Chosen bouncing around the kitchen and immediately pauses and takes a step back, her eyes filled with hurt.

"Cora! You're up! Finally!" I exclaim, trying to salvage the situation.

"Yes. Sorry if I kept you waiting." She pauses, watching my oblivious little morning pest carry more dishes towards the table. "I didn't sleep well last night."

"I'm sorry to hear that, are you feeling okay?" I walk towards her, reaching out, but she keeps backing away.

"Not right now, no. I might just go back to the bunk room and lie down for a while."

I wince, hoping against hope that she isn't retreating due to Natalie stepping all over our plans this morning.

"I'll save you a plate and leave it in the Derde room for you?"

"Sure, that sounds great. Thanks, Ronan," She turns away murmuring, retreating back down the hallway.

Cora

Now that I've wasted the morning away sulking over my competition, I finally force myself out of bed. A hot shower is just what I need to relax and reset the day. A literal fresh start.

I grab a towel and the rest of my wash things from my locker in the bathroom then stop on my way past the mirrors. Turning towards them I examine my reflection.

I'm hot, right? Like, girl next door hot, at the very least? Right?

This is why dating back in Derde sucked. The endless swing from 'am I good enough?' to 'they are incredibly underwhelming' is exhausting. I know I'm considered conventionally pretty, with my dusting of freckles, brown eyes and jet-black hair that I keep cropped to just above my shoulders. Pretty, but practical.

Walking over to the showers I turn the handle to make it as hot as I can, filling the room with steam as I prepare to be scalded into oblivion. The luxury of a hot shower is not wasted on me after growing up homesteading. Our rainwater fed showers were never this indulgent, just a way to get clean after a long day.

Finally, I step under the spray and let out a massive sigh as the water pounds into my neck, hot yes, but utterly relaxing.

The door to the bathroom creaks, "Occupied!" I yell as I quickly turn my back to the room. *Fucking glass walled shower, no privacy.*

I wait a moment, listening to see if the person went away or not. No footsteps. All clear and back to my little slice of calm.

Suddenly the steam shifts and I feel someone there. Opening my eyes I see Ronan, towel wrapped around his waist, leaning on the glass shower wall near the opening to the rest of the room.

"Fuck. Ronan. What are you doing?!" I yell out as I move to cover myself as much as possible.

"Trying not to lose my nerve," he whispers, approaching me. "I felt like an asshole for how this morning went. And I wanted to make sure you knew that you're the only one here I have any attraction towards. The only one here that I want to pursue anything with." With that he slowly undoes the knot at his waist, letting the towel fall away.

I suck in a breath, trying not to stare, but most definitely failing.

"Is this ok? Am I totally misreading this between us?" he asks tentatively.

"No. No you aren't misreading it. I just... I'm just not very experienced," I mumble, trying not to appear the picture of misery, admitting this to him in my vulnerable, naked state.

"Then let me lead." He pulls my hands away from my body, grinning coyly, and presses me up against the wall with his torso.

I can feel every ridge of his abdomen, pressed against me, and his very impressive length below that. My face feels hot, my back is chilled by the tile and my pussy is quickly responding to his nearness. I press my legs together and feel the slickness collecting at the top of my thighs. *Oh, hell.*

"Tell me to stop if I do anything you don't like." I feel him whisper into my ear as he starts kissing his way down my neck.

"I don't think that'll be a problem," I croak, my voice going in the wake of all this distraction.

"All the same."

Ronan makes his way further south and licks at my nipple before sucking it into his mouth and biting down gently. I let out a moan and my back arches, giving him better access.

"What should I do?" I ask, breathless and panting as he continues to torture me softly with his mouth.

"Nothing, I just want you to enjoy this, Cora." He gazes up at me as he goes down to his knees on the shower floor, sinking onto his heels and leaning in close.

I bite my lip, unsure of what he's planning and then, very quickly, I find out. He tenderly kisses my mound and then uses his fingers to spread my lips, licking at my clit.

My head rolls back and knocks against the wall. "Unh, Ronan..." I grab at his hair and pull him against me, never wanting this to stop and he pauses, chuckling.

"Doing okay up there, Cora?" he teases, continuing his delicate licking motions that are quickly spinning me up, chasing my oblivion. My anticipation grows as my legs tense beneath me. I can't find it in me to reply as the pressure builds in my pelvis and I feel as if I'm going to burst.

Ronan extends his tongue further, nudging at my core, before retreating slightly and sucking hard on my clit. My vision goes black as I come forcefully and rock into him, holding on for dear life.

"Holy shit, Ronan," I murmur as he slowly gets to his feet, leaning in to kiss me.

"Are you done, or do you want to keep going?"

"There's more?!"

Chapter 5

3 Weeks after Arrival in the Cria Zone

Ronan

I roll over, notice that Cora's climbed in with me again and slowly wrap my arm around her waist. As I scoot closer and nuzzle into the hair at the back of her neck, I realize how peaceful this feels.

Waking like this, wound around her, my heart is full to bursting. Her chest rises and falls smoothly as she lets out the lightest of snores and it just ruins me for anyone else.

Seeing her so peaceful just emphasizes how much she must be overthinking while she's awake. I decide to tease out those worries to help smooth her brow permanently from here on out. She should never have to carry the weight of her mind's tricks on her alone again.

"Ronan?" she mumbles softly, turning into my chest and curling up there.

"I'm here, go back to sleep, babe," I whisper into the top of her head, scratching my fingers gently down her back.

She cuddles in closer, tucking her feet between my legs and I breathe in deeply, trying not to flinch from how cold they are. *Classic.*

CHAPTER 6

1 MONTH AFTER ARRIVAL IN THE CRIA ZONE

Cora

Now that it has been a few weeks since Ronan and I started sleeping together I've decided that I'm just going to permanently claim his bunk as mine too.

I waffled for a few days, worried that maybe I was moving too fast or being too clingy, but so far, he hasn't seemed to be bothered. If anything, he seems quite happy to have me close at hand for some sneaky middle of the night fooling around.

I can't say the Chosen with bunks close to us are quite as happy about my choice, but fuck it. I'm staking my claim.

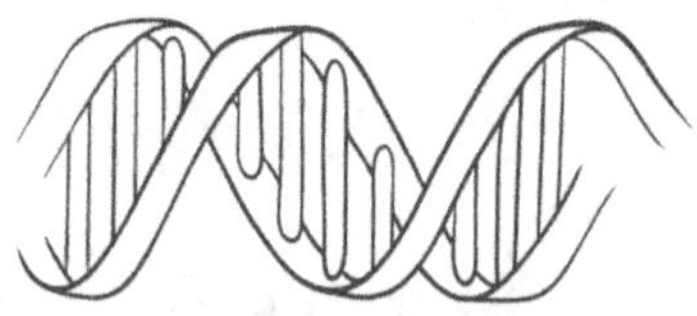

I walk into the bunk room with an armload of laundry, intent on changing our sheets after Ronan came in dripping from the pool this morning for a cuddle. To my surprise Natalie is just sitting on our bed, as if waiting for someone. Given that I've been camping out in Ronan's bunk I'm more than a bit shocked.

"Can I help you?"

"Oh, hi, Cora. I was actually searching for Ronan. Have you seen him?"

Shit. Are we really doing this?

"Not in the last half hour," I hedge, feeling a flush creep up my neck as I try not to get upset at this poor girl.

"Hmm, he told me to meet him here when I ran into him earlier. Maybe he just forgot." Her face is crestfallen.

The heat is building all over my body now, and my hands are shaking slightly. I throw the laundry down and spin on my heel, leaving Natalie without an answer.

What in the actual fuck is he doing meeting some other girl in the bunkroom in the middle of the day?!

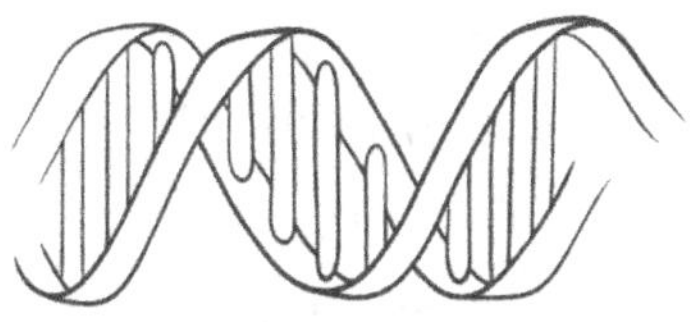

"Ronan. Do you have a moment?" I interrupt, finding him hanging out with one of the other male Chosen on the deck.

"For you, always, Cora." He smiles at me and unfolds his lengthy body from the bench to follow me around the side of the compound. "What's on your mind?"

"Please cut the shit. Why was Natalie waiting for you on your bed in the bunk room?"

"Shit! I completely forgot about meeting her. I hope she wasn't upset!"

"You're worried about Natalie being upset? I'm upset, asshole!" I nearly scream. I'm trying desperately to keep my cool but utterly losing it in the face of his nonchalance.

"Cora. I was going to meet her there to try and help her out with James without letting him in on it. He spends basically all his time outside and the bunk room is the only room without windows that we could meet without him potentially seeing us. She didn't want him to think she was into me."

I let out a massive sigh of relief but my stomach flips as I realize that I just called Ronan an asshole for no reason.

"You do realize how it seemed to me, given I wasn't in on this little plan though, right?"

His eyebrows shoot up and he covers his face with his hands, bending over at the waist and cursing under his breath.

"Cora. I am so sorry if we upset you. I honestly didn't think it would be a big deal. I was just happy to help point her in a direction that wasn't me after that breakfast clusterfuck a few weeks ago."

"Well, it did. But now I feel a bit silly for blowing up." I turn away and shake out my hands, trying to rid myself of all the nervous energy I've built up in the last half hour.

I feel Ronan's hand land on my shoulder, as he pulls me into himself and rests his chin on my head.

"Cora. I feel awful for putting you in a position where you didn't trust me. It won't happen again."

My back goes all warm with him pressed against me and I feel my emotions cooling as I let myself lean back against him.

"I promise I won't call you names again, that was inexcusable. I don't want to talk to you in that way, even if I'm upset. It wasn't okay."

He squeezes me tightly for a moment and then spins me around to face him.

"Deal. We can be better, together, in the future."

Chapter 7

5 Weeks After Arrival in the Cria Zone

Ronan

I pull myself out of the pool, dripping wet and search for my towel. It's not sitting where I left it on the stepping stones...

"Who takes a towel?!" I yell, convinced that one of my housemates is just fucking with me.

I hear a giggle from around the side of the house and immediately run in that direction.

Cora is standing in the yard holding the towel, waving it at me and smiling deviously.

"Oh, this old thing? Is this what you need?" She laughs, spinning to jog away from me.

"Oh, no you don't! It's cold out here!" I take off running after her and she squeals as she picks up speed, trying to outrun me.

Cute. But *no chance.*

I let out a whoop and sprint towards her, catching up quickly. I skid across the grass unable to slow my momentum and we crash into each other, promptly landing in a pile of arms and legs on the ground.

"Ugh, you're getting me all wet!" Cora wails, trying to wiggle out from underneath me.

"I do tend to have that effect." I smirk at her, grinding my pelvis into hers and making her blush.

"Ronan! We're in the middle of the yard! Anyone could walk out here!"

"True. I don't think we could do anything to shock them though at this point. Hormones are running high in that compound lately." I chuckle. She squirms again and I feel myself getting hard as she rubs against me. Cora stops trying to escape as she notices and peers up at me through her lashes, testing my willpower.

"Well, unless you want to make the extent of our relationship incredibly clear to everyone, maybe we should move this somewhere else?"

"There's an idea," I say, keeping my body solidly on top of hers. "We should make this official, don't you think?" I grind against her again, fully erect and feeling needier the longer we lay here.

"Pause. Just hold on a damn minute here. Are you trying to tell me you want to officially pair up? While literally on top of me?" she squeals indignantly.

"Well, yes. I've been wanting to for a while but now is a good time to discuss it." I smirk. Her heartbeat quickens against my bare chest and her breasts are damn near to escaping her v-neck tee shirt with my weight shoving them up like this. It's such a distracting view I catch myself shifting my body slightly to pull the shirt further down, wondering if she'll catch me.

"Hey, eyes up here, Ronan!"

Shit.

"Hey, I've said my piece. I'm waiting on you sweetheart."

"Are you serious?"

"As a heart attack," I deadpan.

"And you thought this would be the way to ask me?!" She slaps at my chest in mock outrage.

"Well, I'm not exactly good at being romantic on purpose, so this feels on brand for us." I snicker, leaning in to kiss her.

"You're impossible, you know that?"

"Still waiting."

"Yes. Obviously. Yes. I'll officially pair up with you, you big oaf." She rolls her eyes at me.

"I love when you give in to me." I move my arms up to cage her face between them, leaning on my elbows to show off my swollen biceps.

"I love you... Shockingly," she relents, throwing the towel over us and giving into the kiss.

"I love you too, Cora."

CHAPTER 8

2 MONTHS AFTER ARRIVAL IN THE CRIA ZONE

Cora

We have to wait until the second supply caravan arrives to report our pairing to the government. The governor that arrives with the monthly supplies is thrilled and says she can't wait to report the first official pairing upon her arrival back home.

Ronan just hauls me up into his arms. Spinning me around and generally making an ass of himself in front of the governor while I get embarrassed enough for both of us.

"Thank you, Governor, would you be so kind as to post our letters to our parents so they know as well?" I yell over my shoulder as I'm being spun around.

"Of course, dear, just ensure I have them in hand before we leave and I'll take care of it. I'm sure your parents will be thrilled to be welcoming such a strong young man into your family."

"Yes, I imagine so," I whisper, catching Ronan's eyes. "Ready to homestead in the Wastes, babe?"

"With you, love? Anything," he breathes in my ear.

AUTHOR'S NOTE

Aww, Ronan, the sweetest and most calming boy. I could spend forever writing about him. Cora on the other hand, was very therapeutic to write. As someone who experiences anxiety myself, her journey in this book was so lovely to share page by page.

Since this is a prequel short story, you get to live in this world even longer!
Turn the page to see all the books currently available in the series.

OTHER WORKS

The Mating Grounds

Chosen for You
Our Year in Cria
Paired Off
Falling Double

Heartland State

Frat House Summer
Love, Lectures & Lava Cake

P.S. All works are written as interconnected stand-alones within their series and can be read in any order.

ABOUT THE AUTHOR

Ciree Hawthorn is a voracious reader turned indie author. After swimming laps in the creative job pool—working in fashion design, being a small business owner, and trying her hand at illustration—she thinks writing is the calling that suits her best. Born and raised in the Midwest, she now lives in the Pacific Northwest with her husband and their two dogs, Arya and Ripley. The whole crew is usually found cuddled up on the couch watching sci-fi movies or out playing pub trivia.

www.ingramcontent.com/pod-product-compliance
Lightning Source LLC
Chambersburg PA
CBHW072125150726

47999CB00005B/2130